HUNGRY
BLACK HOLE

by Andrew Wilburn

The Wilburnness

For my nieces,
Megan, Aspen, Aurora, and Emily

*In the light
of a moon
a massive star
sits on the verge of
collapse.*

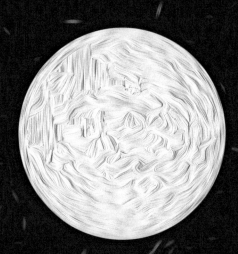

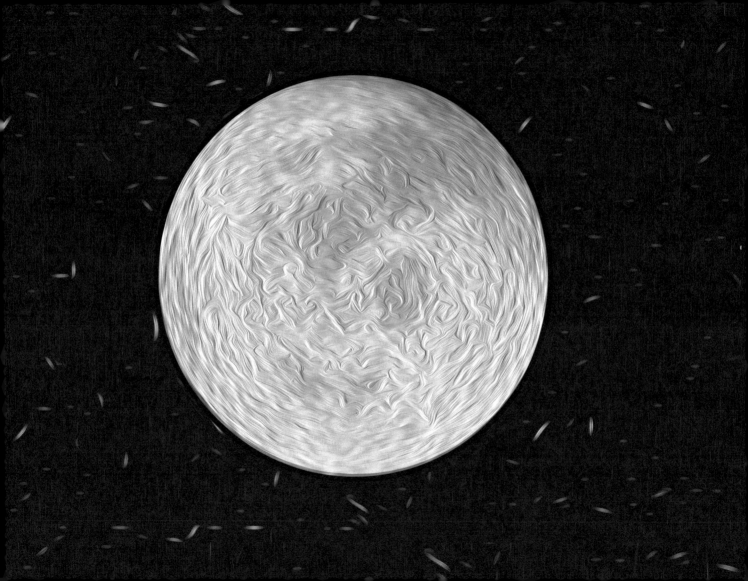

One Sunday morning the star fell in on itself and -pop!- out of the star came a tiny and very hungry black hole.

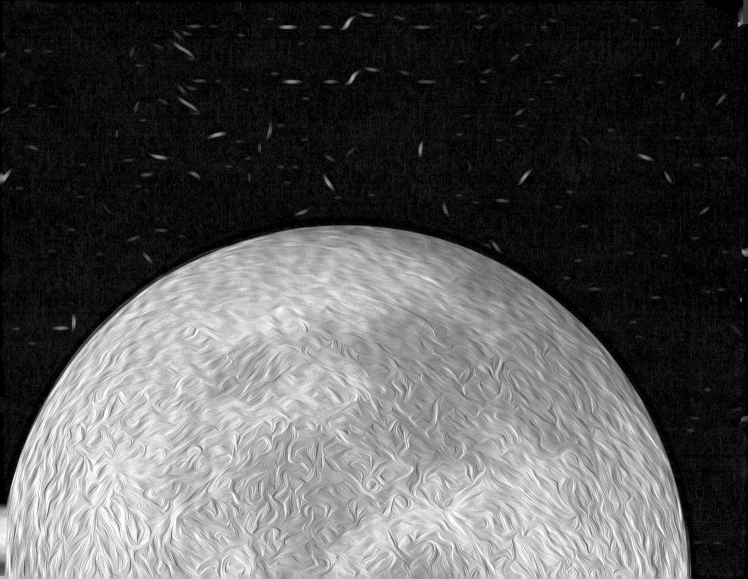

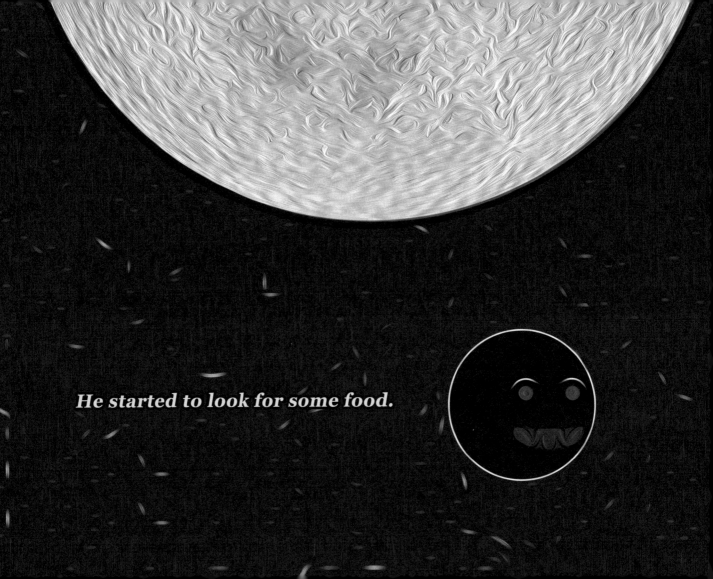

He started to look for some food.

On Monday
he ate
one comet.
But he was still
hungry.

*On Tuesday
he ate
two moons,
but he was
still hungry.*

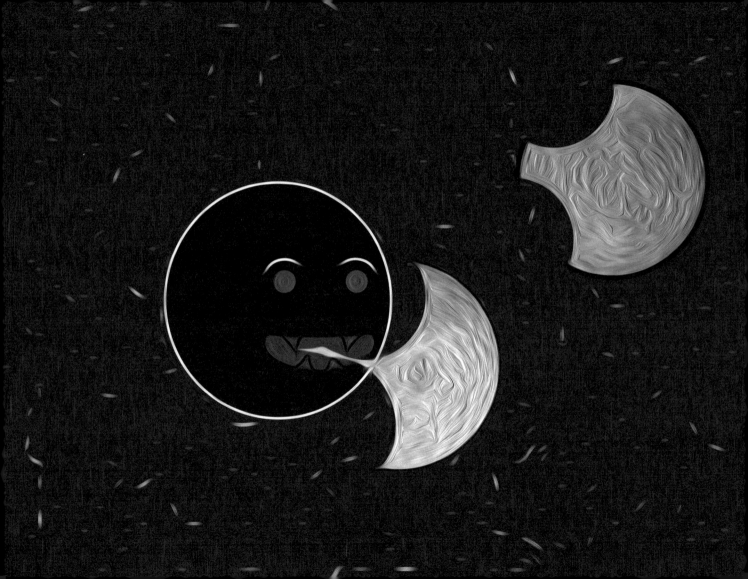

On Wednesday
he ate
three dwarf planets,
but he was still
hungry.

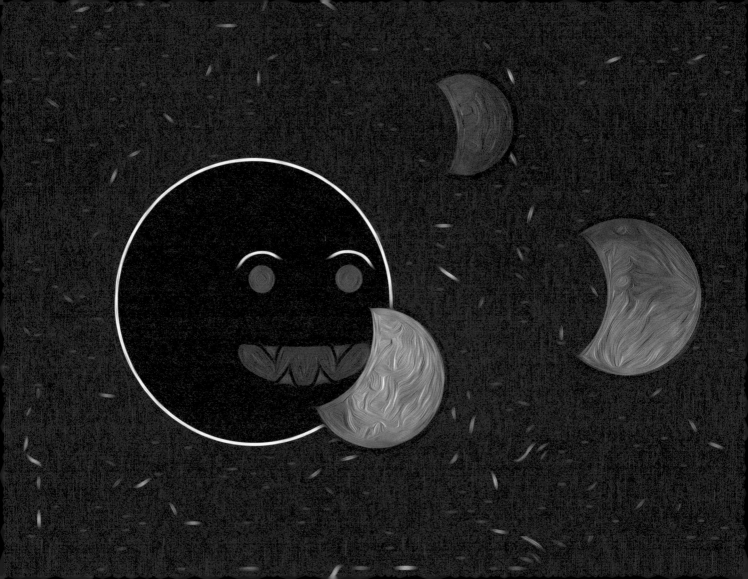

On Thursday
he ate
four rocky planets,
but he was still
hungry.

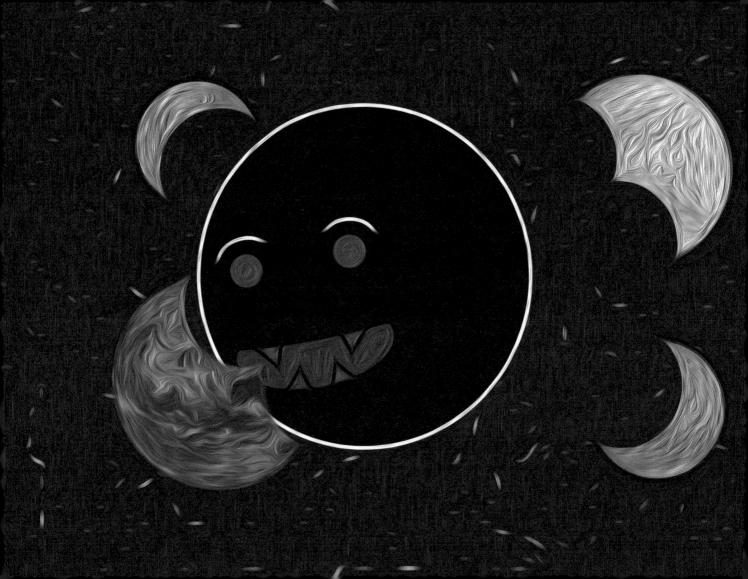

On Friday
he ate
five gas giants
but he was still
hungry.

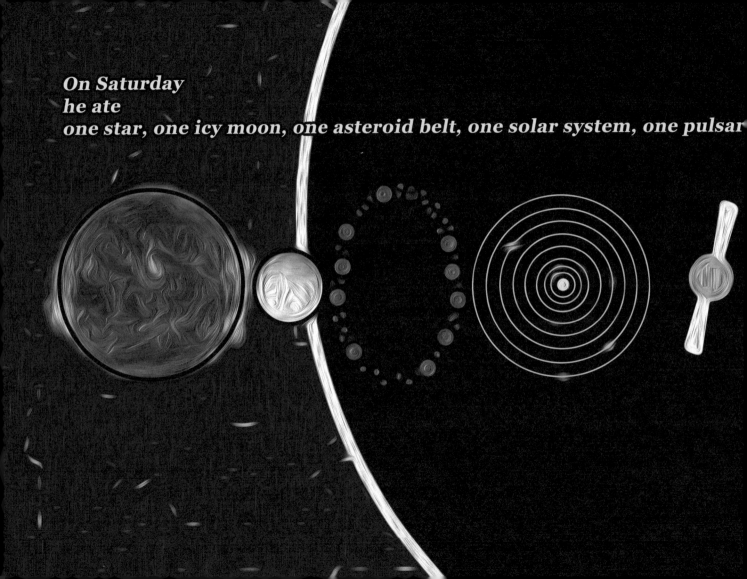

On Saturday
he ate
one star, one icy moon, one asteroid belt, one solar system, one pulsar

one quasar, one blazar, one nebula, one galaxy, and one galactic cluster.

That night he had a stomachache!

The next day was
Sunday again, the
black hole ate
one nice asteroid,
and after that he
felt much better.

Now he wasn't hungry anymore - and he wasn't a little black hole anymore. He was a massive, fat black hole.

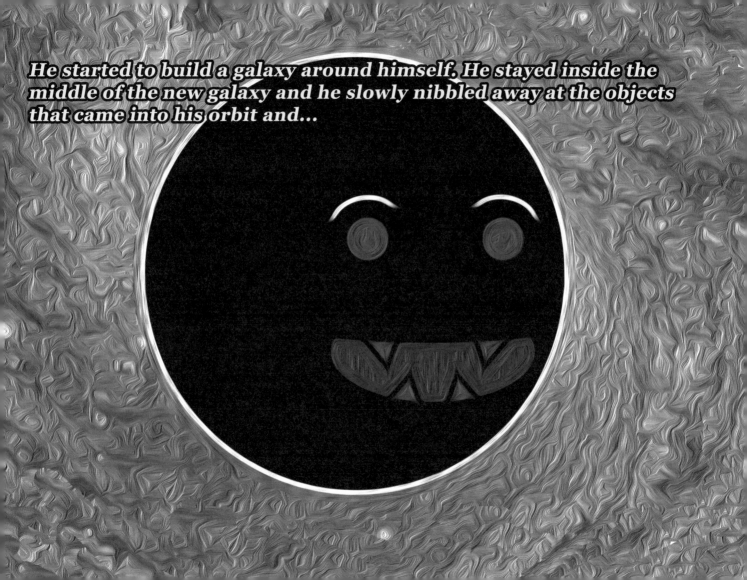

He started to build a galaxy around himself. He stayed inside the middle of the new galaxy and he slowly nibbled away at the objects that came into his orbit and...

he became a beautiful super massive black hole at the center of a spiral galaxy.

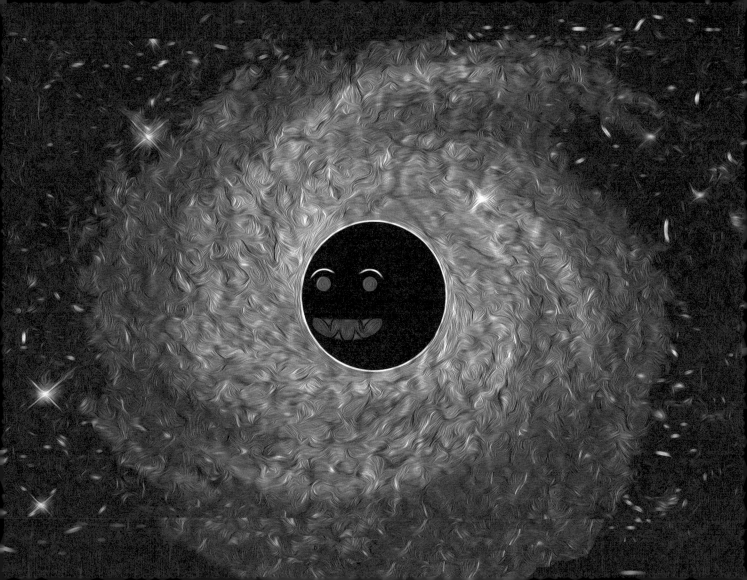

29613630R00017